RHYTHM OF SOULS

REASONS AND LAUGHTER

FANATIXX PUBLICATION

FanatiXx Publication

AM/56, Basanti Colony, Rourkela 769012, Odisha
ISO 9001:2015 CERTIFIED
Website: *www.fanatixx.in*

"RHYTHM OF SOULS"

By: **SRISHTI A. KUJUR**

ISBN: **978-93-89106-88-6**

English Poetry

1st Edition

BOOK FORMATTING: JAPNEET KAUR

BOOK COVER: ISHMEET SINGH

PRESENTED BY: REASONS AND LAUGHTER

DISCLAIMER

This is a work of fiction. Our editors have tried their best to edit the content of all the author/authors and check the plagiarism. All the write-ups in this book are unique and are only published in this book.

In case any plagiarism or error is found, only the author is responsible alone, and not the publisher.

ACKNOWLEDGEMENT

My gratitude to all the writers who have contributed to this book and making it a reality.
My heartly thanks to Japneet kaur the founder of reasons and laughter who gave me this amazing opportunity and encouraging budding writers all around the world.

I dedicate this book to all the readers, who might find their perfect note in this world of mistune and make a beautiful melody out of their lives.

May every page you turn manifests the fullness of life and helps understanding the differences around you to make this world a better place.

COMPILER

SRISHTI A. KUJUR

Srishti .A. kujur is a 90s girl currently based in delhi. She has completed her graduation in the field of commerce from Gargi College DU. She believes that every day is an opportunity to learn and gain new experiences which she would cherish in life later. She believes that every soul on earth has their story to create and here she is hoping to create an amazing one for herself. In the midst of every day highs and lows she is here to find her perfect note to create a beautiful melody.Attachments area

FOUNDER

JAPNEET KAUR

Japneet Kaur, daughter of Mr. Surjeet Singh and Mrs. Dilpreet Kaur was brought up in Indirapuram, UP. She is pursuing German language and BA programming course from Delhi University. She is a passionate writer who loves to pen down her emotions and environment and strive to make her parents proud.

She is even working on her very first novel making her one step closer to her goal.

Instgram : @sheedreamss

EDITOR

PHALGUNI JAGADEESH

"There are many ways to achieve something in life and knowing the purpose of living, I got mine through words."

A budding writer with a passion to learn more and improve. A happy soul, finding peace through writing. Co-authored 35+ Anthologies, Compiled 5 +anthologies, Head Compiler, Marketing & Social media Head of Reasons and Laughter writing community. Invented two poetry forms named "TRIALPHA" & "QUADSY" ehich is published in a blog of "Writerstolli", a writing community.

Instagram : @phal_candy

DESIGNER

ISHMEET SINGH

Ishmeet Singh, a 20 year old undergraduate from Hanumangarh, Rajasthan. One thing I am passionate about, is writing. A massive potterhead, loves to read. But one thing I hate about myself is being a master of procrastination. I literally find it challenging to agree with anyone, making me a bit annoying sometimes but if I like you I am gonna be as loyal as magnet to iron, just one of my hufflepuff traits i guess. I can have a conversation about anything for hours only if you can indulge me in one.

Instagram : @hufflepuff_pride7

QUOTES

RHEA BOGARAPU

1.Shower me with the
  blissful petals of your soul,
  with the essence of your warmth
  and the feeling of your lips
  against mine.

2. If only every
   poet had a muse
   like you, art would be
   in abundance.

3. We waltzed across
   the cobbled streets,
  lost in each other's eyes,
   dancing our worries away.

4. We were doomed from the start.
    Hasn't history already provedthat star-crossed lovers
  never make it till the end.

DEEPSHIKHA KUJUR

"Joy Ride"
On the back seat of a bike, I took a peaceful ride.
Starring at the moon, while it was hiding behind.
The breeze touched my skin and crossed my face,
Giving me the strength to take part in life's infinite race.
Every time it came near it told me to live, enjoy and fly
above the sky!!

"New Me"
Started off somewhere, without knowing the places well.
Packed my bags and stepped out of the comfort without
ringing the bell.
I was running away from the dark in search of dawn.
Who knew it would bring happiness and bright day light
with the different me.
So much better, so much lively, I found a beautiful new
me!

"The wait"
Waited for him with every beat of heart.
With a little doubt and hesitation within,
I wished for him with every shooting stars.
That he will say someday:
"I am yours and you're mine."
With my hopes lingering!

"Express"

Break the monotony, try and express.
Let it out, all that's lingering inside your head.
Dance, Sing, Write or Speak.
Remember it's important to share.
Because, in today's age genuine feelings are rare!!!

NIKITA GUPTA

1. Stop holding grudges against anyone in
   your life because it's like holding an anchor
   and jumping into the sea. If you don't let it
   go, you will drown.

2. Life is all about troubles, worries,
   compromises and sadness. So just forget
   about it and make a living because it's all
   about smiles, laughter and happiness.

3. Stop comparing yourself to others because you
   have to become a better version of yourself
   not of that person.

4. Stop explaining yourself to others because
   if someone really wants to understand,
   then they will understand you by your
   silence you don't need words to make them
   understand.

NIKHIL GOD

1.Pain is what I have been drinkin'
 Why I have been livin'
 That's what I have been thinkin'
 Scared that I am sinkin'
 and maybe I am...

2. Everyone deal with their own insecurity
   Hoping that I hit maturity
   Fuck the world and all its obscurity
   From the demons inside, I need security
   Even the holiest were born with impurity

3. All Eyes on me
   Trust nobody is what I do,
   Don't try to stick your lies on me.
   Solitude is a win-win,
   I wish no one cries on me.

4. She said,
   is our love enough?
   I said it can never be
   Cause if not now,
   When will it ever be?

NAVNEETH .K. ARKA

1.Inch by Inch, gently,
  You have filled my heart
  with an ocean of love,
  quenched my soul and
  disappeared like rain.

2.Like the moon
  that wanes gradually,
  I want to take away all the pain
  You are feeling
  Without letting you know.

3.And when she thought,
  It would be a mess ,
  To be with him, he apologised,
  then did she again,
  fell for a lie.

4.And I felt,
  the pain leaving my body,
  as I realised,
  everything stayed
  only for a time being.

ARUN TIRKEY

1.Straight line is an artwork. Adding highs
   and lows creates a masterpiece. Don't be
   harsh to yourself, add a bit of rhythm and
   your lows will become a beat to it...
   Which will turnout to be a melody!

2. I won't be able to remember my yesterday
    until I go through my memory lane of doomsday
    or smooth roads of highway.
    Cherish every moment and convert your life
    canvas to a masterpiece.....
    As life is waiting for you to be the master
   who can create a beautiful altarpiece.

3. Every night curiosity in me arrives...
    Leaving an unanswered series of questions
    and just seeking for some suggestions.
    I know, I don't have any answers for them....
    But my heart interrupts "Ahem Ahem!!"
    Let's once again fall for them.

4. I don't know what will work, what will not,
   so confusing....
   Feels like bulbs of my brain are fusing.
   However it's my house of decisions.
   Where I am the architect, you need not worry
   I'll manage with some repositions.

SUGANDHI

STORY

1.There's a story behind
   everything. Sometimes
   we play the character in
   that story and sometimes
   we became the audience
   of our own story.

2. It's ok to feel the
   pain sometimes.
   It brings you closer
   to the person who
   offers you medicine
   to cure the pain.

3. We all experience
   the feeling of subdue
   in our life. while some

flow with it and some
   learn from it.

4. Writing is not just painting
   the black canvas with ink.
   It's a creative journey
   for the writer since his,
   every new experience gives birth
   to a beautiful thought.

MICRO

POETRY

PIYUSH PAWAR

"OBLIVIATE"

I'm fading through time,
My shadow disappears into the oblivion as the dawn
breaks across the desert sky And
embraces a new day ,
Will I wake up to see a new dawn ,
Or will I fade away with the morning breeze ,
Will I ever hear the wind chimes sing in rhythm as I walk
through the raked up autumn leaves,
Or will I remain a memory ,
From Today , until eternity !

MOHAMMED AHMED

22

"BEAUTY IN DESTRUCTION"

You know what is simultaneously beautiful and
melancholic?
Watching a defeated storm unravel and fall apart like an
exploding star.
Baring witness to empty endless stares searching for
sparks in the blank spaces between deep breaths of silent
cries.

VANAM NADASHREE

"SHADES OF LOVE"

Frozen by the warmth of foggy clouds,
Will melt and drip as a hailstorm
In the heart of ocean ...
Love,
Detect me and hurl at the sky.
I'll be a queen of stars
To move in the rhythm of salsa
With barefoot on the edge of waning crescent.
Darling, let the night king whisper our endearment
Till the end of trillion galaxies.....

PRATEEK BISHT

"TIME"

Time shall beautifully paint the sky blue,
Let the sun shine bright,
So does it shall also bring the stars & moon out,
Because darkness too needs light.
Seconds were the longest in grief,
So were the minutes leading to hours,
Days would feel like years passed,
Joyous moments may seem shortest to last.
Autumn shall let the leaves fall,
Only to rise & bloom at the springs dawn,
Time holds this immense power to heal,
Patience shall bring back your zeal.

<u>SUMITA LAKRA</u>

"Those times"

I just want to go back to the times
When I hugged you for the first time
When I came forward and knowingly lost myself in your arms
I just want to feel the same feeling again
When your cheeks softly brushed mine
When you kissed me for the first time, out of nowhere
When you first held my hands, unknowingly forgetting the whole world around us
When your hands rested on my waist and my arms around your neck
I just want to relive those moments
Again and Again.

"Footprints etched in the sand"

Amidst the sand dunes ,he stood still,
he could feel a sandstorm and a whirlwind
within him, as if sandy whirlwind vortex,
the whole landscape was enveloped in
dust and sand, natures fury was at the peak ,
swallowing all in sandstorm,
after the destruction it caused in his life,
the storm within subsided,
leaving him with dusty eyes filled with teardrops ,
the only remnant was her deep print
of footsteps in the sand.

<u>POETICALLY BROKEN</u>

With just one glimpse of you
I saw glitters in your eyes
The sparkling desires trapped inside
The shivering lips waiting to be kissed
The perfume of your body that smelled like an unnatural
scent
The sound of your breathing way too loud
Just as if a thunder in the cloud
With just one glimpse of you I fell in love
But how?

MOHAMMAD AMIRUL

ASYRAF

"A Little Thought"

I seek to hear an old song,
About the joy of blossoming orchid in the rain grow strong

The train of thought rushed heavily on sleepless night,
But hold on to sunrise that will shine so bright

Let the tears of yesterday be kept in memory,
Walk up straight to escape and roam free

The fate of future is not within our hand,
Just unveil our mask and conquer our land

At times where dollar sign is king,
Reach out your arm for the carefree it could bring

ASHISH VERMA

"IMAGINARY EMBRACE"

A fountainhead
Of unimaginable pain
Erupts in my heart
To imagine us embracing
Under the moonlight
Imagining your heart beating
Against my chest
Crumbles my mind
Into a bottomless void
That can never be filled
By your memories

RIDA E ZAENAB

1.Dear broken hearts! I've been through many highs and Lows . Sometimes I find myself questioning "Why me ?" .Or that "My life could be happier ". I know most of people been through the same shit . When we start talking about our problems they start talking about theirs . But we forget that our body and our heart is designed in this way , the more we suffer , the more we pass through difficult times , the more capacity it creates for the upcoming troubles. The more we've through the more strong we become. This is what you need to understand and tell others rather than cursing yourself in front of them.

2. Hello future self ! Don't kill your memories . Don't kill your past it will haunt you. Instead of forgetting   them adore your scars .I know there's a troubles causing through your veins. There is darkness so what ? If you've lost your way imma tell you there are still some lights on. If you cant stand imma tell you there are still some hands out there to hold. The memories of past will fill the places that someone left you with . Don't push them away. Allow them to heal you . I need you to feel okay. Memories will remind you not to make foolish decisions in future . So don't kill your memories . Don't destroy yourself .

3. Hello! To all kings and queens out there , Whenever you are crying , thinking to quit everything or having suicidal thoughts , just go and look yourself in mirror . Stare at your red eyes and realize the fact that you are on hell if beautiful creation of nature. Recall what you've been through. Think of it from the start . Think of how brave you are that you've made it this far . Yell at your reflection and tell yourself that nobody and nobody but only you had these nerves to bear all this pain and you are the one still standing . You are no less than a king . And believe me you'll see your eyes dried up. Don't ever forget the fact that you are an amazing person , a king indeed .

4. Garbage thoughts .
Isn't this ironic that
We kill a flower Because
Its Beautiful.
We cage a dog
Because Its loyal .
And we kill us
Because we find ourselves
Not beautiful.
And we cage ourselves Because
we find others not loyal .

POETRY

SRISHTI A. KUJUR

"Bluff"
Falling apart each day
Trying hard, to win
At this wretched game.
Is where
My innocence was lost.
In this world of gamble
My naive heart
Couldn't hold absolute love,
Anymore.

Where people change hearts
As often as their closets
Those feelings, they alter
Mix matching,
To follow trend.
And those sugar quoted talks
Are only there to succumb
Those lips spilling lies
Are never without a cause.

And those huge skyscrapers
Built on concrete of lies,
One adores, with all their heart.
Forgetting,
In this world of gamble
All they know
Is how to,
Bluff !

"Grey clouds"
This world, was never grey.
Until..
I met you, I realised
In darkness ,I laid.

The love i found
Has made me gold
This heart, once lost
Has found shelter, in you.

So I bring my baggage
Unpack my feelings
In your bed.
Dress, and undress myself
In Front of that mirror,
That stands still near your hallway.
Or at times, i can help you clean
And throw away, your mess too.
We can share our long carried griefs
As much as our happiness under one roof.
And when the storms break,
Carrying those heavy rains, above
I promise I will hold you close.
Waiting for that rainbow,
That colors the sky
Just like you did,
When I carried my grey clouds.

SHJLANAND MJNJ

"STONES"

At the Seashore, waves of
happiness touches my feet;
But the Sand feels rough to me,
as the heart still aches.
The Earth feels Unearthly to me,
as the Cunningness it carries within;
Walking wounded under the stars
gives me hope, & with shattered
pieces I walk alone.

Watching It twinkle, I step
on mute Stones;
Melody of the Sea gathers me,
Calming my veins it renders me;
Courage is all I seek,
Knowing it lies within Me.
Every stone paves the way,
For the Forth coming Perfection;
Conquering hate by changing ways,
Coz chances of Salvation is not there always.

PALLAVI BORAGAON

"IMPERISHIBLE"

With a sneering smile on your face
you proclaimed me outdated
for my age
With your words, you abase
declaring, my victory is an apparently
unattainable illusionary race

But, I ask this
do you envy the original adroitness I own?
or, you are afraid to get your absurdness
out in open?

Since you know,
you can never surpass the crown
of wisdom I own.

And, I tell you this
As I age,
I will be enhancing at every single stage
and like the classy vintage wine,
with passage of time,
I will be more polished and fine
Entrancing every man out there
with my fineness
I will incandescently forever shine.

SHRADDHA KOSARJA

"FORTY TWO"

Faint shape of all things spent
When the world was just a playground
Life was just a game
The lost races threatened to catch up
And I was no longer the same

So I put down my arms
And submit to their norms
Shut myself in a box
To weather these storms

Incinerated again and again
At the altar of my desire
Everything essential to survival
Just as surely drowns me in holy fire

Learning to embrace the fall
The most erotic tango of all
Ambition and arrogance, want and greed,
Bread and gluttony, to love or to live?

You once asked me
Why I laugh at the worst of times
Do you see the madness of life?
Does this explain my crime?

If all that keeps me sane
Is being enslaved by these chains
Is love not worth the pain? Is life not worth going insane?

NYONIKA GOSWAMI

"CRUSH"

Brown tables turn rainbow,
Blank pages suddenly turn blue,
No letters walk straight on lines¬–
Flying and dancing with every thought.
Each tedious task becomes a bliss,
Every day the mirror sees the excitement behind that
smile
Ah! This is beautiful indeed.

I suddenly become a detective, a researcher, an optimist,
a believer,
Always looking for that bright star–
A star that shines only for me;
When others strive for it, I rage in jealously!
I seek when the brightness hides;
I adore the colour it wears–
Always hoping for it to remain same.

I pray for your happiness,
I look for that everyday smile,
I desperately wait for you to speak
This is care, a care that you aren't aware of,
And you will never be.
This will not fade but you may;

This is genuine, but you are silly
This is beautiful yet painful;
This is one-sided, this is crush.

PRANUVE

"HAIL TO MOTHER EARTH"

High in the serendipitic sky
Stagger the incomplete charismatic clouds
Racism is an awry failure in the eyes of our Mother
Revamped are the dating-back-history brought-ups, qua a
Broad-minded epitome of vision stands the accidental
daughter of dust and gases

Blacks, the warmly welcomed
Whites, the fraternity ever admired

Both the harbingers of peace
One a benefactor of farmers' grin
Other a visual treat to the eyes of tired wayfarers

Like mother like sons
Humble and modest everywhere
Grateful as ever
Hail to the Mother!!!

SHANATH

"LET ME GO"

Thousands of thoughts running amuck in my head
And no one in the world
Cares to understand one.
You pass by me
And don't even notice.
I pass by you and I can see your whole life
And your world is a world I will never belong in,
And I will try not to.
But you expect me to have results same as yours.
But I am not you,
Not her,
Not the person you would want me to be.
I am a shadow fleeting by,
Burned by the light,
So desperate to hide.
Let me go.

I understand when I look at you
How this is all you need,
A haze of days tangled in weeks,
Where you eat knowledge
And exhale not a word of your own.
I understand you will cure the world
Of its constant ailments

And I respect you,
That is your world.
But I am not you.

Let me go.

I breathe, I breathe
I live by seeing, feeling,
By laughing, by watching the strangers
I don't have to befriend
Or isn't of the same house as me.
I live by people,
People whose world is built by wood and chalk

And the dust flies likes ember ,
I live by their world
And get some dust on my face
And I breathe in their blood.
They are the people I want to be with.
Let me go.

Don't get me wrong
I respect you,
I do,
But you don't like me
And I don't like you
And I don't think
We should do the same thing.
You are a block building a bridge
I am a wild flower lost in the wind.
Let me go.

ISHEETA JAIN

"THE FLUCTUATION OF LIFE"

A machine monitoring pulse rate
With lines graphically high and low
Indicating the existence of a life

Be it periodically fast or slow
The moment it's balanced and static
The constant leveled line won't bend
And that's how each one of us knows

It represents "The End"
Life was never meant to be
A simple straight line sight
It is supposed to rise and fall
Every day and every night

Gracefully accept life's flaws
They're accompanied by its strengths
Let it teach you the way of being
Let it carry you to far-sighted lengths.

SOWMYA VANGALA

"CHANGE IS INEVITABLE"

I failed number of times ,
Yes , I was depressed .

I felt worthless of living
Even judged myself .

I hold back myself ,
For really long time.

I doubted my talent ,
and it was at verge of ending .

Then started my inner voice,
Saying I don't deserve this.

Then started my gut feeling,
Saying I need to change .

I couldn't be what I was anymore,
For what I want .

I started to change slowly with
Help of nature and surroundings.

Many things still came in the way ,
Blocking the road .

And with every storm that broke me ,
I learned to shield and go forward .

It went by many days with
Highs and lows
But I never left positivity
And still I'm going forward
Unknown destination though
Loving the journey and learning life .

ANASUYA BARDHAN

"WHERE DO YOU BELONG"

You stand there alone,
In a crowd of known
For you do not belong there!
You belong here,
In the rays that light up the sky,
every dawn.
Amidst the serene breeze,
spreading peace.
Hymning with the birds
Dancing with the petals of every flower.

You belong in the flames of a raging fire,
spreading warmth
and in your profused sweats
That tastes of your day gone
long!

And with the night
As the moon dances with your shadow
You rest on your lips,

With a resilient smile.
You lie in your dreams
Floating high with the clouds
Raging against those high sloped mountains
Wishing to be like the myriad of stars-
Glittering up the sky above.

SHREYA VERMA

"RISING"

It's dark. It's pitch black.
The cold wet hands of the dark
Take me in it's arms,
Holding so tight and
So temptingly.
I do not open my eyes and if mind, too afraid to see the
never ending darkness
That surrounds me.
I try and try and try but the arms holding me do not want
to let me go.
It gets hard after trying countless times
To get to the surface,
Being stuck in dark days, dark thoughts and the dark
ocean.
The things that used to make me happy
Don't have an effect on me anymore.
I hopelessly try to hold on to something,
Think it's special.
But then I realise, it is just
Water, like every other particle around me.
Nothing special.
It gave me hope and then broke me in a second.
I shut everybody out but let you in.
Then why did you break me?
How can I not pretend to be okay,
When people around me

make it so easy to?
The shadow seems to lure me towards it.

Willingly now.
It wants me to give up trying to get to the surface.
It hurts trying again and again.
It couldn't be bad to just rest and
Let it take control?

The thoughts, the insecurities,
The weight of mistakes I made,
Try to take me to the bottom.
This void makes me so numb,
I don't know who I am anymore.
I want this to stop.
Its ironically gentle hands with tender touch,
Seep through me,

Through every wall I built around myself,
To just leave the black footprints of it's fake promises.
Tainting me for life.
Will I ever want anyone to break my walls again?
The darkness of my mind engulfs me more than what is
outside.
The dark resonates through me.
My throat burns with the untold feelings and desires.
My lungs are ready to give up
And welcome the darkness within
With warm hands as his are cold.
I scream but only it hears me.
It seems to enjoy every second of it, laughing at me.
I am no longer familiar
 with the beauty
Of outside and inside.

Just dark.
But I try to rise, for I still have life left,

I still have reason to keep breathing.
Me, my dreams.
In this dark and oblivion world,
I have to be my own saviour,
My own rock.
So I will rise.
For even if there is a slight ray of sunshine,
Little bubble of air and hope,
I will not give up.
I choose not to be weak anymore,
Scared anymore.
Like these depths of the ever so majestic and dark ocean,
I have my secrets.

These secrets, these flaws, these thoughts are mine,
And I will fight. I deserve to live on the life
I planned for myself since my childhood.
I have not been through all this to just
Give up and fail without fulfilling my wishes.
The ray of hope and light guides me towards the surface.
I will spread in my stance,
Keep my head high, and aim for the sky.
The darkness has to go, it has to leave.
And eventually it does fade.
The surface is not far now,
But battle is won,
But the war of the lifetime will go on.
And I will fight everyday,
As I owe it to myself to live on.
Giving up is not the solution.
And when I surface the water,
When I come out the other end,

I emerge from the darkness and show it,
How it cannot overpower me.

It can never overthrow me,
Not today, not ever.
My damage is beyond repair,
but I will put myself together
Piece my piece.
I will make myself again in new image
And a better one.
I will dive in you again and again depths,
And will conquer you each time.
I will come out better than before.
I will always get above you
And always will be above you.
I am a survivor.
I am me.
I own it, and I am not afraid to rise.

MOHAMMED AHMAD

"THE SEARCH"

I have stopped running blindly.
It's not living, on the run.
The deluge of pain always
swallowed me.
I have stopped questioning why?
It's not fun, waiting for the silence
and symbolism. The truth was always
transparent; I was scared to face it.

I have concluded wondering;
it's suffocating and secludes
the excitement of tomorrow
and the potential to grow today.

I am living in the unlimited existence
of the moment. I let the serendipity
guide me. Tomorrow's fortune is as
gracious as today.

I muse for the silhouette of endless happiness,
it is my reason for living, this heart is pierced
and this soul is bloodthirsty for passion.

I seek no more than a few moments

of honest tranquility and eloquence
that will enlighten my entrapped mind.
Dearest spark of enlightenment resurrect

my compassion and desire to live.

MICHELLE TIRKEY

"SHE IS A REBEL KIND," I HAVE HEARD ALL MY LIFE"

As a kid I did not sleep at 10pm
Like most of the other children of my age did
I wouldn't listen to elders most of the time
Because doing something half heartedly didn't make sense to me
I'd feel I was being told to do something because it's only meant to be that way
And would keep wondering if anyone ever wanted to find answers
"She asks too many questions," they always said.
But they failed to notice, I did not feel afraid of ghosts or dark
I did not hesitate talking first, with new kids across the street
I did not cry on my first day of school
I'd run, and play, and fall, and still not cry
Even when I would want to
No one understood why.
I painted the skies red, waters green, leaves yellow.
I was wrong, they said
"How can imagination be wrong," I thought.
In high school, my friends dreamt of meeting their favorite actors
Or to upgrade their wardrobe with the trend

When our geography teacher taught us about Northern Lights

I blurted out in excitement that experiencing it was in my
bucket list
"Only in your dreams", everyone mocked me
But I did not understand how could dreams be unrealistic.
Now I see people of my age fulfilling their bucket list
Five countries before 25, for some
A car before 30 for others
I don't know if I still have a bucket list
Or a clear vision of what I want
A cup of coffee and the hues of the sky makes me feel
content
They say I am too dull
And I still don't understand why.

Maybe I only wanted to be different
Not a rebel
I was only a kid
I did not know what being a rebel meant
It made me feel bitter, the word
I was becoming something I am not supposed to be.
And now the word rebel has started to make me feel good
May be I will always be this way
As if it is a friend I had made in my childhood
The only constant that has, and will stay with me always.
This is a story I don't want to call mine.

KEITH ROZARIO

"Life - The Journey Of Rhythm And Beats"

Life is like the eternal syllables
They remain forever with us
These syllables are never constant
They are parallel to the infinity

The quantum source of these tunes
Are the rudimental instruments
That give meaning to our dead lives
And keep us at bay from the polluted world

The force that supports our downfalls
Is the secret behind these soulful rhythms
Ask an artist about his first love
He'd swear it on his music

Music itself lies as the intermediate
Between the soul and body
The perfectionist as well would fail
For the soul truth lies on the fact

The true music comes from the heart
Which serves as the purpose
Of freedom pride peace and honor.

AYUSH THAPA

"Rhythms Of Life"

Walking through the streets, of empty and of may;
From the red to the greens and to that old places of grey.
I wonder how it changes, when and where?
These rhythms of life with whom else do I share?
The jazz kind of days that drag me through,
The blues hit the night time when I feel blue.
The love that fills up this "hillbilly" kind of heart,
These rhythms of my life, when one ends the other starts.
The caresses of my worries, my carelessness when happy;
At some point when the notes are dull my rhythms of life
are crappy.
But when at ease and this heart is pleased, I sing my songs
of great;
Sometimes the rhythms go up and down, and sometimes
the lines are straight.
The soulful turns of the rhythms I follow, like in music into
life;
Walking along the turns as said, walking long to thrive.
With these melodies of lessons learnt, you and I shall sing;
The songs of early morning sun and how the victory bells
shall ring.

TANYA KHETAL

"LOST SOUL"

In the world of darkness and dullness.
She finds herself lost like a river running into an
unknown sea.
Standing alone with her own sufferings and misty eyes,
she seems to be lachrymose.
She wants to step her feet out and hug open-air .
She is surrounded by her own bewildered thoughts
like handcuffs around her wrists.
The gloomy situation doesn't depict her weakness
unless she lost her hope.
A glimpse of spark makes her eyes charming and striking
The day is not far away when she will break all the
shackles
and comes out as a new born baby to mark her own name
in the pages of history.

"LOST SOUL"

YAKSHITA RAWAT

"BEEN A WHILE"

From where to start?
The talk of my heart.
Because it will never stop,
Your name being on the top.
But what I say, is it worth the heed?
Do you feel the attention I demand,
Is what I need?
Or
Are you too naive to understand?
Or it's just your habit never take a stand.
Perplexed and clumsy is what you call,
But I've been this way forever don't you recall?
Too close, too soon?
Or will it be gone by the noon?
Can't live with these misunderstandings is what you said.
Wouldn't it had been better to fix the problems instead?
Is it me who is failing to understand?
Or is it you who's letting things slip off his hand?
You expect me to understand you,
Without you uttering a word?
What do I even do?
I just want to be quiet for a while,
For you to decide is this even worth your while.
Because I am hell sure about it,
Only if your heart would permit.

Or maybe I should just sit somewhere off the shore
playing with the thoughts in my head, and making castles
of sand.

Because what I feel is way too deep for you to understand.
I've seen the highs of love,
And ofcourse the lows it shoves.
I've seen myself becoming nothing to his everything,
How he changed from overwhelming to a heartless being.
Love is quite powerful they say,
But still I feel so powerless the same day.
Want to say a lot which is entrenched deep inside
But what's the point? So just let it hide

The sun doesn't seem to shine any sooner,
But that doesn't mean you ought to live like a loner.
The powerful might turn powerless,
And all of it might just make a mess.
If not sooner maybe a little late,
But the sun will shine right out of my gate.
It could be brighter,
I could be wiser.
It might cause a burn,
But that's exactly from where I need to learn.
Making the tables turn
Living without you has been a difficult ledge
But now here I am right over the edge
My love couldn't teach you not to escape
But oh my love! You had me by the shape
However it got dismantled
How easily I was sampled
Maybe It's not sounding right
Maybe it shouldn't

Because even you had choices
But you just couldn't...
Couldn't stop me from leaving
Left me all alone grieving

I feel you never thought of apologizing
For the ruckus you've been disguising

It's all the happiness initially,
The happiness trods down to ignorance, eventually.
Never thought you'd reciprocate the way you were doing,
You won't understand but everything is ruining.
It's not about a fucking period of time,
All I want is you to be mine.

The days are just passing, and the nights passes by too,
What lasts eventually is the thought of you.
You want your space I'll give it to you gladly,
Just don't leave me alone, I'll keep wondering madly.

People call it hoax,
But I still hold my hope.
Everything will be fine soon,
And you'll again love me back to the moon.

Going back to the good old days,
In the winters behind the Hay.
Right outside the mall
Sitting on the stair,
The way our eyes stall
And my hands playing with your hair
That was my happy place
I found peace in that one big gaze
You held my hand like you'd never let me go
And even when I did once you said please, no.
And in that moment I realised what happiness looked like,
It just went away, all the stress and that fright.
Your nose is the best part,
But you smile resides in my heart.

You said that you loved me like you've never before,
That your love was deep till the core.
All the memories that we've made,
Bursted out just like a grenade.
Left me all wounded
Leaving me shredded
I guess you like it this way better,
And maybe that's why to you it doesn't matter.
The way we were I simply bow,
The love we chose is not how it is now.
It seems like you don't care,
But still I feel there's something missing in your air.
Does my absence bothers you?
Would you ever again say I love you?
Why does my poetry has to be gloomy and sad?

When our love wasn't that bad?
I wish you let go of this ego and agony,
And come back once again calling me your honey.
But in the end it's just a wish,
Maybe someday it'll be a bliss.

Longer the time passes by,
I ought to take a deep sigh.
Never thought I'd come this far,
Alone, when you left me apart.
Weren't we "meant to be?"
To me it was the epitome of my glee.

Distressed and broken heart,
Shed me to several parts.
One stands up to you,

The other against you.
What's wrong what's right?
All of it turned to my fright.
You still exist in my head,
In the dark nights,
the tears soaked in my pillow on my bed.
It comes back in flashes,
All the memories you burnt down to ashes.
I hate you for you did,
Left my heart to forbid.

<u>SHAES</u>

"I LOOK FOR SONATA AMONGST THE SYMPHONY"

I plug the earphones on
Trying to hold back, yet to move on
The melody starts; starts anew
Takes me on a journey unlike a few

The myriad notes play
one by one; very slow
Spinning the melody, amongst
the highs; and the lows

Being embraced and engrained
Letting go of the world that feigned
As I ponder about the life;
the soul which was in a slumber; did rise
Discovering insight;
through these euphonious eyes

If there is a high there might be a low
If there is a low; it won't always stay the same you know.

I reflect back;
As I continue to hear
the melody starts to break the trance
of all those incessant horrid fears

A residual of chaos
Still waiting to disturb the harmony
Yet;
I look for the sonata Amongst the symphony.

ZEHRA ALI

"WATCHING OVER ME"

Whenever i look up at the sky
I feel someone talking to me
i feel i can see you looking after me
i feel i can talk to you too

whenever i look up at the sky
there is a feeling of peace
there is a feeling of stillness
there is a feeling of a kiss on my face

whenever i look up at the sky
i never feel too rushed
i never see flashbacks
i never rewind the past

whenever i look up at the sky
it makes me cry
it makes me full
it makes me smile

SRUTHY S. MENON

"VANILLA TWILIGHT"

Walking beside the lanes,
searching for the favourite playlists ,
those flush of memories,
just like the sudden gust of wind,
propelled my stranded thoughts,
drifting me across the night sky.

Every twilight,
when I yonder to the skies,
I longed to see you
a wish, just to be with you
where, you can watch me
from your paradise.
To know me
Though_
myself a stranger
than a friend or a foe

MONICA TOPNO

"ANGEL EYES"

With her first hopeful sight
Increased her strength, aiming high
Gave birth to a powerful desire
A desire to fly

She spread her wings
Had just started to take on her ride
But was pulled down, crushed
By her demon's pride

She acknowledged behind her
Demons stronger than her will
Carried on to pull herself free
The demon's wouldn't leave her still

Again and again she would try
Failing each time as we say
At last, stood there wondering
If she could follow another way

Looking straight in the demon's eyes
She leaned forward and hugged him tight
And along with him for the last time
Her wings opened, to a successful flight.

DEEPLEKHA SARKAR

"MYSTIC COLOURS THAT FALL"

Why do I expect more than you can bear?
While the world is moulded by a brutal care.
Our dimensional dreams come true not.
A sudden euphoria is expelled leaving it's spot.
Everyday I try to craft a better than before,
But it always runs from my door.
Though the lighthouse lantern guiding my way;
Telling me to not to fear and not to pray.

I've finally realised, All these mystic colours that fall,
Sometimes being a stardust star & sometimes a fireball,
Are the part of our own galaxy.
Like a constellation craft & not a fallacy.
It's a colourfull creation,
A blessing, that is beyond restoration.

"WHY DOES THIS ROAD LOOK SO EMPTY?"

I'm walking over miles and miles,
Numbers of pedestrians passed by, since I left.
They were also alone,
Though I was with them.

Some talked about lives,
Some talked about fame.

Some shook Hands
Some left some gems.

None ever thought of vows,
None ever tried to support.
If they were with me,
Why do I feel so alone?

I had to leave behind all,
Took not even a single pot.
A long way still left now
I'm tired though I'll not stop.

"WHEN A FLOWER DRIES IN A GARDEN"

Unbelievable, How the man left all behind!
Left his family alone, helpless, orphan.
Two sweet fruits were born from two rare flowers in this
garden.
Now they are seeking for that shield they were protected
by.
Who will look after them when they'll need a shade under
this sky?
Who will spread that fragrance of their talk When they'll
cry?

Maybe he tried.
He tried to hold on a little more.
They say, "He has decided time for every creature He
made."
But was it really needed to call him back so soon?
Leaving this garden before a calm afternoon?
Leaving all his behind that is only his own?

NAVNEETH .K. ARKA

" Love is in the sky"

Oh my dear beloved,

How do I tell thee, The love I have towards thee,
For me you are a sasoning salt that brings taste to the food,
Without you, I would be dried up
as the land which beareth no fruit.

Oh my dear beloved,
How do I explain thee,
The love I've towards thee,
Love doesn't change with seasons, though it is struck by
cyclones and floods,
but it remains deep within, just
like a seed that endureth forever,
beneath the ground.

Oh my dear beloved,
Like the flood which taketh away all the wrath from the
earth,
You taketh away all the pain from my heart but
only with a subtle smile.

Oh my dear beloved,
I would choose you over the moon
that giveth me light in the night sky,
as the rays of the sun that kisseth me hard on a mid day,

and those countless stars in the dark sky,

though, ready to fall, but,my love toward thee, will remain forever.

PRADEEPTI SHARMA

"WHEN THINGS GO WRONG"

When things go wrong,
I wonder, "Is this the destruction the wind of righteousness
did? "
And then, the tempest of emotions swipes away my
senses,
And I am trapped in a gloomy whirlpool of resentment and
guilt,
All attempts to come out of this quagmire go in vain,
And I rest for a while, tired of this eddied existence,
I contemplate the inevitability of everything wrong,
And realize the worthiness of being right,
And do away with resentment and guilt,
Finally, emerging, though gradually,
As storms do not last forever,
Though they change everything,
But what does not change is one's righteousness.
And I feel elated the way I survived the devastating
tornado,
But never lost my righteousness in the process.

ASHISH VERMA

"WHILE I REBEL AGAINST YOUR MEMORIES"

I walk on grass brown and green
Bare feet wet with fresh dewdrops
In cold winter evenings
I pass by the jasmine
The fragrance reminds me
Of your serene essence
The drops precipitate on my eyelashes
Mix with my tears
I try to breath the cold air
Choke on it, exhale sigh of emptiness
Will it always be here?
This emptiness, the void that you left
A continuous feeling
Of being pushed into oblivion
Will it never leave my existence?
This uncanny feeling of not being able to exist
A distant melancholy sound of cello
Reminds me of your flawed smile
That used to light up supernovas in your eyes
I walk, rain pours quietly
Tapping on the leaves
As if applauding the way I feel
Applauding my emptiness
As if I deserved it
I remember the times

When you used to hold my hand
During those long evening walks
And out of the blue kissing me

As if it was going to be our last
I remember you kicking your feet
Away from your body to throw your heels
High in the air and sliding your naked feet
Towards me in the water with force
As if the water would carry your love
And splash me wet with the living force inside you
And it did, watching you dance in rain

Carefree, calling me to join in
But expecting not to
So that you could put on a show
For me, to fall for you
And I did, I fell hard
Immersed myself whole
In a mad dance
With a crooked stance
In chaos
In eros
In labyrinths
In instincts
In emotions
In commotion
In viciousness
And wickedness
I dove headlong
Into your game of love
That you played with me
I listened to the song

With lies on your tongue
When you swayed with me
There wasn't a chance to wake up

From all this into consciousness
But I did, and saw you for who you were
Without my tinted glasses on
And without your masks on
That hid you from me
That cloaked the darkness
Within your soul
I woke up alright
I woke up all okay
But something was amiss
I had lost a part of me
My innocence
My ability to trust
A part of my soul
Forever lost
In the whirlpool of your madness
You couldn't stay to make sure
If I was still breathing
You had other plans

Other victims
Other shows to put on
For those who would come
After me and take bits out of them too
To patch your own torn soul
To sew yourself together
But still never would be whole again
I walk the lonely streets
In cold winter evenings

To heal myself from the bruises
And scars that you left
While you danced with my existence

With a knife in your hands
And I thought it was just an adventure
But it wasn't, I fell for you hard
Mesmerized, gullible, and letting down my guard
But I am awake, I am healing now
And you weren't worth all this
Not even worth the words I write
Rebelling against your memories.

PINA .S. SHAH

"HUES OF LIFE"

Life begun not so harsh,
Remember being in my mother's arms,
Cocooned from the relentless world outside,
Sweet lullabies and in caresses I abide.

And then I grew up and realized,
That the world outside was very cruel,
The loving and sheltered life was snatched,
When God decided it was time to scratch,
And my loving mother was fetched.

Suddenly all alone in the world bereft,
Being strong was the only choice left,
Taught myself and fought my way back,
To the top where I belonged,
Mama said, " You're a princess and
You'll rule the world one day.

So here I am taking the world by storm,
Just like how Mama would have dreamt.

SWAGNIK SAHA

"DOWN THE MEMORY LANE"

As the bus rides along,
The crowded streets.
The optimist rides along
To seek for care.
An emotion he has not been close
For a long, long time.
The sky seemed dark and gloomy
As the downpour was near
Downpour of sadness and emotions.
All seemed illusive.
And the darkness longed for daylight.
The paper boat sternly wanted to stay afloat,
But the stream made it mushy and delicate.
Having emotions was a curse,
Thus the admirer chose to be reticent.
Taking all the battered feelings with pride,
The sunset believed to be calm.
As it was innocuous for all.
The soldier embraced all the bruises,
Than others to be agonized.
A jerk made him feel

That the bus came to a pause.
And suitor came down pragmatic as never before.

Alesinloye Ibukun

"ESCAPING HELL (INNOCENCE)"

She saw alhaji and papa giggling
Like school girls on the playground.
Concerned but too young to understand,
She tried to listen in the background.
Pretending to be full absorbed with helping
Mama in the kitchen.

Alhaji walked towards her,
Occasionally, throwing his
Agbada over his shoulder.
He walked with a limp,
Like he had Glass In his slippers.

She tried to find papa,
Scanning the environment, she found him
still seated on his rocking chair.
He waved at her, Mouthing the words
"It's okay", with a big smile on his face.

"Hello, my dear", Alhaji said,
as he stroked the side of her face.
She stepped back a pace,
When he tried to hold her in warm embrace.

"Good evening sir", she said still dazed.

She smiled, Like the good girl mama raised,
She wondered why her papa wasn't running
To save her from this snake.

She tried to see if papa was on his way But he looked away, quickly, to avoid her gaze.

MADHVI

"RHYTHM OF SOULS"

Life is like a roller coaster ride,
Without any instructions to guide.
Rough ride on two parallel rails,
The two rails of life long scales,
Rails of passions and perceptions,
That ends with wisdoms n lessons.
Well designed with twists n turns,
Pleasure of love or heart that burns.
Precipitous slopes of highs n lows,
The slopes of happiness n sorrows.
At inversions of disgusts n wonders,
Perception drives wonders or blunders.
Have courage to face or fear of defeat,
Opportunities bygone will never repeat.
Tranquility lacks throughout the ride,
Just integrity, be the element of pride.
A sigh of crushing or relief in throat,
Thus builds a spirit on various notes,
Where our perception plays vital roles,
Is what we call "The rhythm of souls".

ARPAN VJNEET LAKRA

"Ruins of a lifetime and flowers within"

I walk, I walk on worn off railway tracks.
Small pink and yellow flowers beneath. No man or
machinery has ever seen them.
Untouched and blooming in secrecy.
My heart sinks.
The tracks end abruptly.
Leading me to a giant red wall. Standing alone in this
beautiful wilderness.
Cracks formed due to creepers which grew.
What a strange feeling this gives me.
Of wanting to go to places, I have never been and faces I
have never seen.
Who decides that what you do is right?
The butterfly effect starts from your head and heart.
I lie down on the flowers on the tracks.
Blue sky and clouds going by.
My hands trying to block the raging sun.
I hear footsteps. Someone is near by.
Who are you? I enquire.
Strange feeling isn't it? She asks.
Holding her frock by the end, legs dirty and flowers
beneath her feet.

Strange, so very strange. Never thought that abandoned
railway tracks could look so beautiful.
Yes, I feel the same. I reply.

Never thought that it could make you feel so many things.
She says.
Her eyes staring into my soul. The light strikes against her
pale skin, warm yellow, a glow of a
thousand sunny days.
The wind blows her hair and her frock.
She comes and sits beside me. Now she sees what I see.
Our legs dirty and flowers beneath our feet.
Look, she says. Itching her nose not a big fan of flowers I
must say.
Pointing towards where the tracks would lead. The wall
behind us.
It's not a dead end, I say.
My pupils dilate and there's hope in my smile.
No, she says. It's the beginning of something beautiful and
strange. Fixing her frock and hair.

SHIVANGI KUMARI

"Volatile life"

I had been playing
A sad or a happy role
On the way
As walking down can bring some faith within......

To walk all the way
I should be brave and staut
As their would be
Triumph and disaster treating me all the way.......

As the disaster let me hate
The fate lying within sunrise and Sun dawn......

As the triumph let me wave
The life within sunrise till
sun dawn......

TUBA HASAN

'Tides of Life'

Mind paralyzed
Thoughts blocked
Heartbeats numb
Time is tough
Everything is dark
Time doesn't pass
You saw my struggle
But you won't see me fall
Regardless of downfalls
I'm gonna stand tall
I'm wearing a smile
Though I want to cry
And those deep bruises
Brutally murdered my consciences
Leaving me alone in the dark
The moments of happiness have passed by.
But wait...
The glowing wind will blow again
These dark clouds will flown away
And I'll rise high Just like a bird fluttering in the sky.

OPEN LETTERS

JAPNEET KAUR

"SHE"

To the demons of society,

I m not someone you just fake sweet words at first to claps me later with your filthy hands and spark of barbarian in your eyes.
I am not the one you fake love just to throw me in ashcan later, when your desires are fulfilled or when my sensitive body could not gather enough courage to endure the pain which is given to me by your bad intentions.
I am not someone you can entice to leave me broken and dying in dark in a place not much known to me.
Yes, I am a girl but that doesn't mean that I allow you to break every part of me by not sparing any inch or my body with your lustful hands.
I am a girl with values, I have my own dignity.
I am not a toy you would play with and throw away when you are tired or a piece of shit which, when spill on your shirt, you would just throw it away because of the stain which remains.
I have my own worth and pride.
I am much more than your expensive wardrobe which is of no use.

I am not meant to be used when you ultimately have to throw me.
I am not different, I am just like you.

I have not got two horns on my head or a face not resemblance to human.
I m not just your shirt which once worn become of no use.
I am not a material you would decide to use and throw when you are done.
I have my own self worth, dignity and respect which is priceless.
I am a girl, doesn't mean you got all your rights on me.
Unlike you, I don't need a tag of 'in a relationship' when I know I don't love you or we won't have a future together.
If I say 'I love you' i mean it. My 'I love you' means that I need you in my future, that I want to have a family with you, that I want to share my good and bad timed with you, that I want to grow old with you.
I don't just come in relationship just for a tag or my satisfaction.
I would love you to death or leave you dying, all depends on how you treat me.
I m not your slave who would obey your saying without even thinking on it for a while.
I will not just do anything for the sake of love, because I have my own self worth.
I m a girl, that doesn't give you the right to exploit me.
I m not dependent on anybody. I have my own goals and ambitions.
I have my parents smile as my first priority.

Who gave society the right to tell me that I am skinny or fat because I shouldn't look like that.
I am a brown girl, but that doesn't make me look bad, why should I be sad?

My features are not sharp and that doesn't affect my confidence at last.

I don't have a nice figure but that doesn't make me look any less of others.
I am the way I am, I look the way I look, I love the way I love, I dress up the way I want and these things doesn't make me different from others at all.
I am not easy to understand and this is what makes me look "ME" and guess what, I am proud of it.
I am not a slut or a whore, I am the one you never met before.
I am not a second option because I have the self worth to be the only option.
You cant just spread false words describing me, because I am a girl and that people will believe in you.
Don't try to make someone I am not.
Don't try to change me for you,
Don't try to kill me by complaining about my body structure,
Don't try to defame me because I don't deserve this kind of treatment.
Love me the way I am or get the hell out of my way.
I am a girl with pride not a girl you would leave down lying.
I am not thirsty for love,
I just need you to respect my worth,
I am the goddess you pray to everyday,
Then why you look at me with thirst of sexual pleasure from your eyes?
Why doesn't your hand shiver when you unwrap me to kill every inch of my body and break every piece left with me.
You just can't use me for your sexual pleasure because I am just like your sister and mother.

FROM,
EVERY GIRL OUT THERE

JIGYASA SRIVASTAVA

OPEN LETTER TO TIGER

Dear friend

A long time has passed since I met you but you know what I miss you like hell. We have spent very small time in proximity but you have become an integral and indispensible part of my life.
I am sorry I didn't had a word with you which was my utmost responsibility being your friend and companion. I know you are sad and glum as your survival is in danger. I also know how it feels seeing our children, family members, friends dying in front of our eyes. I can understand your grief. Although I know that we humans have no right to kill those insane animals which are protected by nature's license. But you know what one thing that God has given us is 'greed'.
This is the utmost reason.
Humans are perilous beings, who can terrify and kill even death.
This is really very cruel and barbaric act and I appologise you from on behalf of all the selfish ones. I know you are very depressed that like all one day you will also be killed and Everytime your's and your loved ones life seems to be at stake and I perceive the truth but I promise you by my side that I will do my best to make people realise their mistakes and their sadistic actions .Trust me really I will

do this and tell your emotions among all so that even if some will be able to reach to my words, their essence at least few innocent will be saved.

I know the fact that only 3890of you are left and in that also many are caged in zoo, away from your natural life, where you don't get a chance to grow strong both physically and mentally. I understand your grief but my vigorous efforts are to abolish this zoo system as it is like a dungeon and place of death for all animals.

Being an animal no one to see your tears, your bereavement, your sufferings, they all have just forgotten that you are a living being, a divine creation of God and they are no one to harm. They all have just proved the fact that, " man is the biggest animal, the scariest, brutal dangerous of all."

But you know there are still good people with some humanity left, who build national parks and wildlife sanctuaries to protect you from those selfish ones as those have completely forgotten meaning of word 'human'. I aptly remember when I was a child and went to circus I always asked my mom 'how can a master control a big tiger?'

But now I can feel how your heart must be aching at that time, when you had to act, dance, play games and had to do other more activities just please people and that also merely for survival. I vow you that I will make full efforts, heartedly to save you and your family. Please don't feel bad. Please smile for a while, the world will look beautiful and you will get positivity and hope to live because you know smile is the tool which gives you strength to fight for the right and it changes your perspective towards the world and rest I am always there for you. Remember me with heart and I will be there and

God is seeing everything, he is your saviour, he will punish all the gluttonous ones and he is always with you.

Hope you are happy now and don't worry I will meet you soon.
Yours
Jiggu (childhood friend of circus)

DEVENDRA KUMAR

Dear Highs and Lows,

I would like to thank both of you for accompanying me in this voyage of life. My life would have been nice and simple without both of you. But who wants that... Right? My mind always dreamed about living an adventurous life filled with lots of ups and downs.... Highs and lows.
And that's exactly what happened to me.

First of all, I am gonna talk about lows. Lows are painful, dark and almost impossible to live with. Sometimes they drown you deep into a swamp of fear. The more we try to get out of it, the more we get sinked in it. We start to lose faith in ourselves. The clouds of loneliness surround our souls and shield them from receiving the rays of happiness. When the highs seem too far from us, we just start to gaze at things through a half filled glass of water. Failures tend to spark through our tears. The foundation of all our dreams begins to crumble. Infinite questions bombard our minds ruthlessly. Why do we deserve such horrible things? Why things are not perfect for us? Why this world is cruel to us? Are we doing something wrong or horrible?

But there are two sides to every story... Right?

Now I am gonna talk about the highs. Being high is the best. We feel like 'The Chosen Ones'. Withholding this feeling becomes almost impossible for us. We can clearly hear the volume of our heartbeats elevating with each passing second due to excitement. Our souls take the avatar of a superiority. Our optimistic vibes nullify the effect of negativity. Sometimes we get too high, which makes us unable to see the ground and we forget how it was when we were low. Smirks are converted into wide smiles. We get high enough to dismiss all doubts from our minds. Because of our elevated spirits, sometimes we ignore the possibility of getting bowled out. But when it happens, we cry and blame others.

We need to balance the highs and lows of our lives. They both play a huge part in constructing and developing our character. They both show us our value and status. We need all the guidance we can get from the experienced ones. After all we all want peace right? :-)

So I hope you both will keep continuing the series of adventures which was started from the beginning.
Yours
DevK

APURVA BATRA

|| A NOTE TO LIFE ABOUT LIFE ||

HEY ! Dear Life

A very warm greetings to colourless canvas of life, I might tell you colorless Canvas but yet you are magical, mysterious Shades covered with dark so think (life) lines. I am sitting here in corner of my dark room sipping coffee and thinking about you, remembering the time. You remember once You stole my essence first to tease me and to make me feel miserable and more messy, I was down that time , sitting on the edge of flaws, I was hoping for something magical to happen but then also you weren't merciful to me.
Once you showed me real mirror of reality, which reflects my scars and wounds but life, all thanks to you you also have help me to cover them in front of this world. Under this bedsheet of stars and moon you have always hold my hand and never let me feel alone , you never let make me down, you always show me a way to Ignite fire in me, life These ups and downs of my life are only evidence of existence, these ups and downs are like melodious, magical node to music of life, yet unforgettable and soul soothing, your ups make me fly high in sky with open wings, your downs make me a night angel I will cherish each and every stone you throw over me because you

make me know that, it might hurt but it's worth, so cheers to you, cheers to me, cheers to us together, we share a bond of Life for life. My dear life let's hold hands together more tighter and happily walk forward holding the real essence of life embarrassing scars through time. You have teach me a lot and I know you are going to teach me till end of my life I am ready to learn more from you we will sail together and reach to destination one day.

Life, Your forever student

APURVA BATRA

DEEPTI LAKRA

LETTER TO EX'S

If you constantly have to tell someone that
same exact thing about how you feel and they don't
change it, understand they don't respect you. Relationship
is a bond between the people's that has been changed
over a period of time. Everyone wants a nice and loyal
kind of relationship that they wanted to share with their
partners. But what if a person is always been cheated in
every relation she has been?
On the other hand her relationship always gets low
because in every relationship she is being cheated by her
partner. But one thing changed her life that she was about
to get engaged to one of her friend, they were friends
from the time of her school days. She was happy and
excited that at last after So many heart breaks, at last now
she was about to get engaged. But she did feared a little at
the same time because her every relation was a heart
break for her, she feared that if this relationship would too
turned into one of her past relationships. Both the families
were happy about that engagement, but destiny had
planned something else for her. The guy with whom she
was about to get engaged, he broke off the engagement,
without any reason. And about this only the girl knew
about it not even the families got to knew about it. Boy's
family always asked the girl that what had happened to

her, that she's not responding to their calls or visit them
anymore. How could she say to them about what all
happened, as she's still waiting for the reason. Is it so easy
to break off an engagement? Is it so easy to break off a

relationship between the two families? Is is so easy to abandon all those memories that were shared. Even after all this, she wasn't able to forget him. She hated it, when her mind is telling her to stop loving someone. But her heart can't let go. She somehow started to begin a new by meeting new people and she thought that it's time to start something new and trust the magic of beginnings. She started to build herself from bottom to the top. But destiny still had decided something else for her, the people whom she met where hardly known to others, they knew everything about the girl from the starting and even about her engagement. She used to hangout with them and she got close to one of her new friend. He was able to understand and they used to share their feelings and doubts with each other. For her the guy was like a counselor to her and she literally started to take up his advices and they used to go for date. The guy noticed that she had started developing feelings for him, but at the same time he did told her that he's not the guy whom she should date. But the way he used to tell her this, she thought that he might be kidding, for a period of time they did dated each other, but their was something for her that was eagerly waiting for her. She knew that for the guy it was never a relationship for him it was just a way by which he could fulfill his physical needs. For him being physical was just a need which every person needed and it should be fulfilled whenever needed.

The guy told her that she shouldn't be broken because even after her engagement was called off, she was still strong, so she shouldn't be weak now or should not be broken after knowing all this. She never thought that the guy would treat her like as if she was "submissive". What is it going on a series of ' FIFTY SHADES', the guy gave her all excuses from his side so she could move on or she should still share the same kind of relationship that they were sharing. But this time she didn't needed to hear his excuses or what he have to say for himself. His actions already spoke the truth. This Time she was much more broken than ever, she didn't want a rich man or a handsome man or even a poet, she just wanted a man who could understand her eyes if she get sad and points to his chest and say "HERE IS YOUR HOME". Now it's hard for her to trust when all she have from the past is evidence why she shouldn't. All thanks to those people who knew that she was strong emotionally and mentally but now she's weak and wounded.

To the one who took her for granted.

RINA

Dear life,

I don't have any regrets and complaints against you, but I do have an array of whys for you ,which are unanswered. As my hope and undying love and spirit will never diminish.
Grabbing my bag hurriedly, I scampered out of my office, hailed a cab and reached my usual destination dot on time. All my exertion and dullness faded. Mere sight of him was like an energizer for me. I sat besides him and started apprising him all my day's activities. The only sign of his acknowledgement was he would give a blank stare or gaze at me without uttering a single word. We love each other since school days.It was like a fairy tale for me. Lots of love and care showered on me. But life is never a bed of roses .After our graduation he took me on a long drive, love was in air, memory of that dreadful day, when he was left comatose after a car accident would always haunt me. Tears welled up in my eyes and spilled down my cheeks when doctors informed me, that he can take a day or may be years to come out of his coma, may be not live. I will never give up on my hope and will continue my efforts. Since last four years am hoping for a miracle , as I strongly

believe that true love can move mountains. I know life will smile at me once again.
Waiting in Anticipation

Yours Rina

RJDA SANOBAR

RAHMAN

To all those heard and unheard of...

I may be just 17.
Or I must say I AM 17.
I don't know what makes me write this ! But I guess that
there are certain things you can't really
discuss with anyone.
And when I can't use my words to speak, I let my written
words speak for me!
What better weapon you can have than writing?

Well I've been very observant with my life.
And I think that is what helped me be a practical person.
People tell me how can you be so mature at this age?
And I don't have an answer to that.
But the least I can say is that it's the vicinity that I have
lived in.

Life isn't a movie.
It's a roller coaster.
Every turn will make you scream and laugh.
And you'll be afraid of a hundreds of things
But you will overcome them!
I think that is the biggest lesson that life has taught me.

And don't care about people
They come and go.

Because nobody can remain
with you forever.
Nobody.

So I think I have witnessed enough circumstances in my
life.
And now I can handle my life
With my own thoughts.

SAISHREE

MOHANPRASAD

I still remember the day, when I first saw you without even a blink, when we first looked, we were actually talking with our eyes. At times we get worried, when we don't see each other.. You made my each day. The more we saw each the more happy we were. That smile and the eyes of yours, I would never forget. When your tuitions would get over, I would run to the gate of my house ,to see you through the window of your car, passing by the road. And there your were, looking at me too. It was your birthday. I came all the way to wish you, because we wanted to see each other. And there you were standing, in pink dress, looking beautiful more than ever. How can I forget our talks in texts, each night. There were times when, I requested the shopkeeper, to keep it open for me for half an hour more so that I could recharge my phone, just not to miss my everyday chats with you. Those days were really beautiful because we had each other. I still remember the day, when your tears came out when you saw me hurt. And I Am sorry because I was a fool who never listen to you even for once and I know there is no

time now for us to get things back. I wish I could get back in time and travel my past, where I wouldn't have been a deaf ear to your wants. This would've never happen, this hurts. I cannot get over you but I have to act like I have. Its been too long since I haven't heard your voice, I miss it, my eyes are missing yours, I miss your smiling face which has always been the reason of my happiness and it were those moments with you in the backfield of our school, in our college and in all the places where we have spent endless time together. I can't share this with anyone because I have always been failing to explain my feelings, and I want you to promise me that you would never share this secret, that we have, with anyone but except me.

Co-Authors

She is Jigyasa Srivastava. She hails from Lucknow. She is a Mechanical Engineer. She is a passionate writer She has been a co-author in two anthologies and is currently working in six other ones and in her own book too.

Tanya Khetal Education- B com (Gargi College).
INSTAGRAM ID: *khetaltanya*

I'm Shilanand Minj From Jodhpur, Rajasthan. I'm Doing BBA 2nd from Somani College Jodhpur. My Email is : zeanshan@gmail.com
INSTAGRAM
ID: *luv_shilxx_7*

I'm sowmya from Hyderabad ,
studying 12th standard . I'm an introvert
who fell in love with writing . I
write about positivity , happiness and life .
INSTAGRAM ID: vss_scribblings

Hailing from the foothill town
of Siliguri, Michelle, takes immense
interest in storytelling, with words and
photographs. She writes about everyday
struggles, questions, dilemmas and
experiences, from a perspective that
projects a positive side of it all.

Shanath is an introvert,
trying to connect with people through the
written word. Born in Guwahati, she
is pursuing her BA with english hons. You
can find her on Instagram
@our_hollowed_bones.

I *am Noyonika Goswami,*
currently doing my bachelors degree in
astrophysics at the UK. I am a published
poet, recently published a book named Seeding
Mind. It is a collection of my
childhood poems that i have been writing since
the age of six.
INSTAGRAM ID: *n13_poetry*

Hi! My name is Sumita Lakra,
I'm a simple girl from Delhi and have
done my graduation in commerce. My
no. is
8882377911.
INSTAGRAM ID:*lakra.sumita*

I Name - Deepti Lakra City - New
Delhi Education - Graduated Contact
details (contact number and email Id)-
8826298328, email Id -
alisonlakra@gmail.com
INSTAGRAM ID: *Deeptilakra*

IMy *name is Prateek Bisht, I*
hail from haldwani, Uttarakhand.
Poetry is a coping mechanism for my
struggles
and insecurities, which helps me heal
and regain my confidence.
INSTAGRAM ID: *@prateekbisht_*

PINA SHAH MUMBAI, INDIA
SPECIAL EDUCATOR TO
CHILDREN WITH LEARNING
DISABILITIES. *Contact me at:*
pinashah150@gmail.com.
INSTAGRAM ID:*@heartflicker*

Yakshita Rawat. Delhi/India.
Literature student. 9205751510.
INSTAGRAM ID: *Yakshitarawat*

Hey *there!* I *am shreya verma,*
a 17 *year old student currently in last*
year of school. I am from new delhi and
love to read. I am a total harry potter
nerd and dog lover. Happy reading!
INSTAGRAM ID: *@shrreyaverma*

Isheeta Jain, Delhi. An eleventh
grader, instagram @a_reticent_soul
~Just a soulful and a passionate writer.
INSTAGRAM ID: *@a_reticent_soul*

Shaes Raipur MBBS *graduate* Mob:
98934 66108.
INSTAGRAM ID: *emotion.labile*

*Nikita Gupta Delhi Pursuing
Btech in ECE 8368342111.
INSTAGRAM ID: nikkuchaan*

*Tuba Hasan Nawabo ke shahar se Still
studying A bibliophile
loves to write while sipping tea parallel to
rains.*

*An avid procrastinator and
bibliophile, Rhea Bogarapu's love for
literature has no bounds. Hailing from
the Biryani capital of the world, this
Hyderabadi can be found buried behind
the pages of a book- if and when she's not
snacking. You can find her poetry on
Instagram, @poetryxrhea.*

Monica Topno Delhi based, now
in Ranchi. B.A
INSTAGRAM ID: _oniika

My name is Amirul Asyraf, but
I prefer people calling me Ash as a writer.
I'm from Malaysia, currently
undergoing my internship for Bachelor
Degree study. You can find me on
Instagram with the handle
@poetry_inabox .
INSTAGRAM ID: @poetry_inabox

Madhavi, a Rajasthani Drug
Liscence holder and a married working
mother with a passion to write my heart
out through my poetries....!!!
INSTAGRAM ID:
@madhavipoetatheart

I *am Anasuya Bardhan, pursuing
my* MBA *from Symbiosis Institute of
Operations Management. I write poetry with
the pen name of Hridmajhhare.*
INSTAGRAM ID: *hridmajhhare*

I *am Shraddha Kosaria from
Odisha and can be contacted at
kosaria.shraddha@gmail.com.*
INSATGRAM ID:*byshraddha*

*Alesinloye Ibukun is
a sociologist and a poet. He is currently lives in
Abuja, Nigeria. You can find
his other poems @highb33kay on Instagram.*

I *am sugandhi Gupta. I live in Agra. I'm a content writer by profession along with it I am pursuing my Master's degree (M.com). My mail ID is sugandhi.gupta14@gmail.com, contact no.*

7456972711.
INSTAGRAM ID: *Sugandhi.gupta14*

Hello, there Arpan here. I am a graduate of commerce from St Xavier's College. I write in order to enjoy and explore the everyday things of life.
INSTAGRAM ID:
*everything_is_here_now_*

Just a man of words, A writer of perspectives.
INSTAGRAM ID: *words_said_out*

Rina Mumbai Graduate.
INSTAGRAM ID:
deep_expressed_thoughts

'It's better to be classic rather than being trendy". My name is Arun Tirkey earning a livlihood in Delhi after completing graduation.
INSTAGRAM ID: *Morningstar09*

I'm Pranuve, pen-named myself as Pranuve Aadhithyaa, from Chennai now studying for my CA exams simultaneously doing my undergrad and a passionate inker.
INSTAGRAM ID: *wall_of_optimism*

I'm Nadhasree from Hyderabad
Completed my graduation in civil engineering
and I love to write poetry not
only about love but nature , freedom etc.
Contact details:9000181445 Flat no
102, My castle apartments, Opp lane to
familia hospital, Road no 12,Banjara
hills Hyderabad—500034.
INSTAGRAM ID: Nadhasree_k_ and
peepfolio

I am Swagnik from Kolkata
currently living in Pune for masters. I like to
pen down my life through poems.
I love doing photography and singing my heart
out.
INSTAGRAM ID:stories_of_life7

Nikhil God is an English
Honours student at the University of Delhi.
Residing in Delhi NCR, he can be
contacted through the email:
Instagram handle
@unheardphenomena.
INSTAGRAM ID: @poetrywnikhil.

Hello, my name is Deeplekha Sarkar. I'm from Kolkata. I've completed my B.A. *graduation and I'm trying to make a change in this so called society through my writing. To Contact me e-mail me on deeplekha85@gmail.com.* INSTAGRAM ID: *lekha_the_writer*

Hey, I'm apurva batra, from indore, I'm an electronics engineer, and a poet. I have a page on Instagram named as crypticsoul, I have been writing there from last 1 month. INSTAGRAM ID:*crypticsoul*

I *am Saishree Mohaprasad and* I *belong from Odisha.* I *did my graduation from* KIIT, *Bhubaneswar and* I *can always get connected through my mail,* WhatsApp *or my* Instagram. INSTAGRAM ID:*Mohanprasad*

*A banker by profession, but
loves words more than numbers. Intrigued by
the fine nuances of life, like
music, art, literature, and love. Loves cooking
and dancing. Children make her
joyful to the core. Spirituality and philosophy
define her existence.*
INSTAGRAM ID: *puropoetesa
& an_unsullied_existence*

SRUTHY.S.MENON (23) *is an
Assistant Professor of English Literature
in Swamy Saswathikananda
College,Ernakulam and she resides in
Kerala, India. She is the Co-Author of
"Amaranthine: My Poetic Abode",
"Nostalgia:Story of Past"
and a few Anthologies.*

*I am Rida e zainab from Multan
, Pakistan . I've been writing since 15 . You can't
become the best without
first being the worst. So here I am .*
INSTAGRAM ID: Prosebyrida

Ashish means blessings. I am from Chandigarh and an engineer by profession. You can call me on 8360022163.
INSTAGRAM ID:
poetry.is.mu.ruse

My name is Navaneeth K Arka hailing from Hyderabad City completed his post graduation in microbiology from JNTU, University Hyderabad. Ph No: 7981203652 Email: navaneethkarka27@gmail.com.
INSTAGRAM ID: *awritersd1ary*

Shivangi kumari College student From Ranchi, Jharkhand.
INSTAGRAM ID:*Guptashivangi763*

Hey guys I am Rida Sanober Rahman. I am doing my BA from Mount Carmel College in Bangalore. Follow me on @alive_in_the_woods. I am a very practical and kind person in life.
INSTAGRAM ID: alive_in_the_woods

Yakshita Rawat. Delhi/India.
Literature student. 9205751510.
INSTAGRAM ID: Yakshitarawat

My name is Keith Rozario I'm studying in the 11th standard in Father Agnel School, New Delhi it's been 2 years I've been writing poems and quotes and it has been a lovely journey with words.

INSTAGRAM ID:
the_black_and_white_stories

ABOUT REASONS AND LAUGHTER

Reasons and Laughter, found by Miss Japneet Kaur, is a community which deals with providing services, compiling anthologies, organizing competitions and open mics.

The main objective is to give a good platform to budding writer, to help them grow, even to provide best services and giving wings to their dreams.

Email: ralservicess@gmail.com

Instagram: @reasons_and_laughter